DARK HORSE

B S BHAMRA

DARK HORSE

Part 1

THE BEGINNING

B S BHAMRA

Introduction

The idea of this story begins many years ago when I first picked up the skills to write in fact it was one of my very first story's that I had created it was one of the stories that I attempted to create I wrote this story way back in 1999 maybe give or take a year. Before I became a schizophrenic a paranoid one. This character is Benjamin, This time he is the dark horse I am still creati9ng what kind of super hero that I want him to become what kind of super hero he is this will be explained as we go through story in his mind there are assassins the baddies the bad guys I am creating a character that has attitude all super hero's have an attitude good and bad.

Dark horse aka Benjamin is sitting right in the middle neither good or neither bad. Some times he does bad things as you will read other times he does good things this is all part of Benjamin character I am creating as I write.

Preface

Dark horse was created through an awful experiment you know in the labatory of course he has a child hood and this was what changes him the images that had stuck in his mind the child hood tormenting and the thought that never leave his side or fact leave him this is Dr Benjamins idea of revenge he would help anybody that was in trouble and the local authority are quick to find out who he is, was and who he was going to be. No time to travel and a girl called robin was his sid4 kick which is introduced later in the story.

Benjamins beer drinking and partying comes to an end after being knocked down in a car crash and with his life flashing past him some how manages to beat the machine and becomes the dark horse. With a stranger called Lucy as his side kick. Will Benjamin and Lucy troubles over cease as benjmain as the dark horse kicks ass on the street and with Lucy as his side kick only to find out that his so called gifts of being super fast speeds along dictionary of weapons that had beco0ome a curse with Lucy taking it all in her stride and is looking at her self believing that it was all a gift. Benjmain is caught in too frames of mind not knowing where to go or who to turn to next.

Chapter 1

Benjmain is writing at his desk reports he is feeling board of his work and he is tried Benjamin is a doctor he deals with the sick schizophernics Dr Benjamin was taking big chances big risks he is trying new medicines a knew tablet it was said on its prescription box that they would control weight control and the tablet ws a magical tablets they said that they would bring your weight down it also said on the leaflet not to over take.

Benjamin was single he had the money and the houses he had been brought up the right way he had been brought up wealthy and he was enjoying his life he had no responsibility's. However he was going to become very responsible.

Benjmain takes just one pill and then falls to sleep at his office desk at his office.

Benjmain had been using the tablets for a while he found them sitting on his side in a chinses medicine shop close by near where he lives in fact it was just around the corner Benjamin ais dreaming of the day that he walked in side and found the tablets. At first benjmain could handle it but he greedy he needed them more, people noticed that he had changed not just in his appearance but in his attitude but his personality as well.

Benjamin was now addicted however his treatment was nearly over as one day while walking to his door he noticed that the shop had gone it was no longer there and with it Benjamin's supply of tablets.

Benjamin did not know that he was about to change not for the worst but for the better you would think he was going to change as the Chinese would call it dark horse.

Benjmain does not do the cool and all that suoer hero bull shit he is straight to the point until he finds out who he is becoming.
As he sits back in his office chair i9n the middle of the day it begins as always first the cold sweats can be miss guided behaviour the anxiousness and then the visions.

The paranoia kicks in Benjamin with the mix of everything else starts to crack up he becomes very thirsty. And he needed to drink a lot of water. That did not work benjmain leaves the room keeping his cool whilst moving around the office and avoiding people mostly work mates.

As benjmain clams up cold sweats start over again with a little bit of vomiting and drooling just to top it off.

Dr Benjamin knows theirs something wrong every time he fails to answer to his own condition his sickness which was his super powers talking over him and thinking that he could changed his mind. Dr Benjamin was running out of answers benjmain was in a rush to leave his work place and get home.

Benjmain needed the medicine man he needed his medicine fast. The water worked but it did not last for to long and all the other stuff that he tried which included vitamins headache tablets and the fresh air did not particularly help.

Benjamin was in trouble Benjamin makes it to the door at the medicine mans shop he was so angry he did not knock he just kicked his door open. Only to find that the shop that welded the medicine that he so desperately needed was no longer there. The shop was empty.

Benjmain could not believe it whi would do sucjh a thing that last sentence came from the medicine man in benjamins coniousness." What" benjmain says." did you say some thing".

Benjmains speaks out again he thought he had heard a voice he continues. " is there anybody there".

There was no answers benjmain leaves the shop slamming the door unintentionally the door was closed shut onlyb for it to open again.

Benjamin leaves it as it he is unconcerned and disconcerned ans well as disalusioned of what was happening to him benjmain did not know yet but hye was losing his mind.

As the cold sweats disperse an extremely har5d heavy headache occurs again Benjamin thinks he has found the answer paracetamol again Benjamin thougt6 of the cure only lasted a for a while it looked like to Benjamin that he was on the run form himself.
Benjamin was beginning to change and he was at the stage of changing fast.
Benjamin was at home he was in a safe place he was sat on the edge of his bed cold sweating and not in so much pain and not knowing what was happening to him only to fall asleep while thinking about what he had taken and why his neighbours the closet people to him had just upped and left.

Benjamin needed the old man except the old man was not their and neither was his any of the remedies which Benjamin thought were helping his condition.

Within the next few hours Benjamin condition and appearance had changed over some time. he ws not exactly a muscle man to start with however his body was looking a little more trim and as for his lower body things were looking quite good he had changed too. This so called perfect body was changing and so was his mind to join it too.

He was getting through it by himself his mind and his body were changing he was feeling better within the week he ws feeling like himself again he was normal. Benjamin awakes and he is looking good and ready to go back to work.

He does not tell his boss about his experience his problem because he did not know that he had one yet. Well not a sickness as such there was a superhero to talk about waiting to arise waiting to be under earthed in to the world to created a justice and all the other stuff that they do.

Benjamin was back in his office and he has or is doing good again in fact he had become a little too confident around the lady's in the office. It was not the lady's that was complaining it was his fellow work mates the blokes the men they had noticed Benjamin trans formation.

Benjamin still had not fully recovered he could feel it in his body especially in the stomach he closes his eyes which was an mistake and makes it home just in time he closes his eyes which was no mistake and makes it home just before it starts to starts the pain that he was in.

Again Benjamin knew that nothing could save him nothing not pills water it was tough his mind says he was forced to sit it out he was going cold turkey. And as being a Doctor himself he knew all the symptoms already including the new ones Dr benjmain had began to mature.

As Benjamin starts to write he begins to create him self his thoughts were different his mind moved faster he said in his notes that he felt different and was stronger he did not know yet but he had become bullet proof.

He had become smarter he was thinking differently and he had a thirst for knowledge especially the knowledge of martial arts. His super powers had began to kick in. Benjamin could feel the adrenaline.

Benjamin faces a new challenge he had defiantly noticed himself however his finds at work who had already noticed him said nothing more. Benjamin has to double check he ws in the offices toilet mirror.

Everything about Benjamin life especially his mind and body became exaggerated his whole life was about to change and on that evening he had become dark horse.

A super hero with super powers had awoken Benjamin finally finds his new self a new all Benjamin dark horse has to do is put his newly found powers to the test. This is were benjmain makes his very first mistake believing that he was in control but he was not and trying to save a man crossing the road and then again in a petrol station was also a mistake as he was not yet a super hero that had to be learnt. In approaching a robber which looked like extremely brave but obviously we had not understood himself or his powers as a super hero and his gift of the sleeve.

However when the robber fires his gun at Benjamin one of his super powers kick in the bows and arrows sleeves that appears and block the bullets unexpectedly and are reflected back and hit the robber the favour was returned.

Chapter 2

Benjamin could not believe this what had happened and when he looked down at his newly found weaponed that also protected him he disappears back into his arms it was not to long before Benjamins as the dark horse finds out that he is bullet proof he had armour all over his body and a long rain coat cross jacket. He also had one special gift the spirit of the horse benjmain is told that he must always worship the horse as it was his dark horse it as Benjamin's side kick and it would only appear when benjmain was near danger unless Benjamin summons him.

Benjamin was not too excited he in fact was worried about all the newly formed powers and then te power of the horse it was black with red eyes.
The horse was perfect where it came from it looked like it was summoned through the sky benjmain ahs a

question it and when he does he finds out that the horse was connected to his mind he really could speak to each other through telepathy.

This was something that Benjamin was going to have to get used to.

All of this was happening extremely quickly and as Benjamin was trying to understand this himself as much as possible when he puts it across to his boss Benjamin is fired and loses his job. As the argument could be hard from a short distance as it gets louder and the whole office could hear it and understand it even the public who were close would stop by to hear it.

One of Benjamin friends a work colleague takes Benjamin side as he is walking out of the building Benjamins friend stops him telling Benjamin that she still believed in him Benjamin answers him it was Lucy she holds his hand out and befriends him Benjamin agrees.

They both start a conversation that would continue for not five but the next ten years and properly more as Benjamin discusses his super powers they were growing more the more he thought of them.

However Benjamin was a virgin of his own master full powers the dark horse he did not know how power full that it could be.

Even though lucy was there she could still not see the same as Benjamin it was late and Benjamin was sleeping not knowing that the dark horse was outside slowly summoning benjmain to it.

Lucy was out of town it looked like benjmain was in for a rough night.

Benjamin wakes up to a red ball of fire surrounding his entire body as he is summoned up to the dark horse his partner and side kick.
Benjamins looking cool lucy was not there with them and this time it worked on their behalf Benjamin did not have too many relationships out side of his work but he actually worked in fact he was a bit of a loner which worked out even better no excuses of not being in the house on time and other things at least he thought he would not be able to hurt anybody's feelings over the fact of who he was and who is was becoming.

The fact was he ws who he was and nothing as going to change rhis he was who he was going to be.

Benjamin does not know yet but he is heading in for a battle of his life with three others they were the bad guys Benjamin had not yet been put in the position he was not their to make friends in fact it was the opposite.

As Benjamin is patt8inmg his horse the dark horse they were having the conversation with him they were discussing Lucy.
As they were saying that she would make another good side kick the dark horse is leading the way in conversations disagreeing with benjmain as he is thinking they would be better with out her the horse thinks differently.

There discussion continued well in to the evening and the very next morning Benjamin has to explain to Lucy who was Benjamins only friend apart from the dark horse who he actually was.
Benjamin comes clean Lucy was happy that Benjamin was being honest about and with her and there relationship was saved.

Lucy and Benjamin did not know that they were being followed this was Benjamins fault and he believes himself the clashes with the sleeves that summoned the dark horse for a conversations about how they were going to save Lucy.

They agree that they should of paid attention more attention as Benjamin for the first time takes his eyes off her as she goes missing. The horse has no feelings for anything or anybody and for that subject and speaks to Benjamin telling him Benjamin is feeling sad and upset not knowing what to do.

The horse suggests that they go and find her the dark horse was right Benjamins says he too should go and find her.

As benjmain clashes his sleeves summoning the dark horse right up to him Benjamin has a lot of thinking to do he was also upset himself about what had happened there had to be a reason of it. And for why they if it was a they had taken Lucy.

Benjamin did not know yet that he could call upon the elements two of them lightening and thunder he could call on the planet he finds this out later on in the story. The evening had come to its end and it was now early morning when Benjamin notices the time and had kept him self up Benjamin refused to stop thinking about his newly formed powers and was teaching himself with every thought.
Benjamin was already pushing his mind and he now knows that it could work extremely quickly and quietly it would work even when Benjamin wanted it to stop.

Benjamin understood it quickly it was the horse it was the centre of everything he thought about which was his mind the dark horse which his mind was attached to so it was the dark horse what wa doing the thinking.

Benjamins understood his horses thoughts immediately he thought of his thoughts quickly Benjamin had received two powers the first ws one of listening and the second was his sleeves.

He was going to find out who took Lucy form him very soon. And Benjamin defiantly got the message as his room down town had been broken in to.

Benjamin was nice and tried and needed a new home he has to find out that he too was being followed not just by the police but by an new opponent. A being that believed he was more powerful " Benjamín". the dark horse says. " you are being challenged"
By who was Benjamins answer as his new opponent refused to identify itself it refused to tell benjmain and the dark horse his name. it refused to show benjmain his face.
Benjamin thinks that it could be a friend he was making it up the things that he was saying was making no sense
Benjamin and the dark horse agree that they were being set up. Not just through there minds but physically.. as for all the waiting around they were both getting worried when Lucy captures were not giving in just yet.

Lucy's capture finally speaks it was the being in front of them to Benjamin via a phone call they were requesting money they had made that obvious and that ws it nothing less and nothing more.

The kidnapper s still kept Lucy captive their was some thing else they wanted.

CHAPETR 3

They wanted the sleeves and the dark horse when Benjamins finds out he speaks about it while having his tea in a café by himself benjmain is being watched by the police and hears it twice he had heard the news.

As a detective continues to question the public besides Benjamin he was going to have a close one as Benjamin gets himself questioned he should of moved off. the reporter next to the detective told Benjamin that they had heard of his powers and even more so Benjamin agrees by giving them a story.

Benjamin takes the reporter a side in to a nearby ally way close by benjmain old office was above them he tells the reporter to stand ten feet apart from him.

The reporter was una sure of what kind of story Benjamin was going to give him. He was unsure of what Benjamin was going to do. He looks over to him as if to say what. Then it happens Benjamin summons the lightening just in the ally way away form the public and afterwards shows him the rest his magnetic sleeves which were part of his mind he still used them clumsily they had a mind of there own.

Benjamin proves it again the reporter again telling him to fire at him only to find that Benjamin is well protected as the bullets bounce off him.

Benjamin is lucky as the reporter catches on he tells Benjamin telling him that his story would not be rubbish. As for what he had just seen. And what he ahd just experienced.

Benjamin is practicing his powers as he clashes his newly formed wrist bands appear once again Benjamin calls out with the power as the power of one become two and it was not with out pain. A pair.

Benjamin was just about to clash the pair together however he forgets the words which he has to say to awaken them first the dark horse was told it was the dark horse which has to be spoken first. It takes Benjamin the rest of the evening and then he gets it he remembers.

It was yet another problem answered as he would remember the little saying as he spoke of as the dark horse is busy trying to convince Benjamin that he was the smarter words dark horse he could feel the power of he creatures close by him breathing remembering his bright red eyes this was an incredible feeling and to top the it off the whole concept of speaking to a horse telepathically with good use.

Benjamin and the dark horse were talking as they both have a lot of energy and test the both of there thoughts with knowledge as the dark horse is telling benjmain that he is ready to teach him.

Benjamin had gfrown lighter and had lost weight and in fact he was as light as a feather as light as a paper weight. As Benjamin had noticed him, self he appears he finally agrees that he should pick up his mail there was one later amongst the letters most of the rest was junk mail. He doubles checks the envelope before opening the let6ter after throwing the rest of the mail back on to his floor by his frontr door. The envelope had his name on the front.
with the keys and the let6tter opener .

Benjmain was looking for his paper knife but still he refuses to open it call it paranoia as he puts the letter back on top of his key table

Benjamin was not interested in opening the mail he was not interested in fan mail that's what he always called it. He still thinking about what he had and what was happening to him.

He needed to communicate with Lucy was having big troubles.

Benjamin was of to the shopping centre he wanted to know how it worked with everything that had gone on he was changing and it was a challenging which was a good thing as benjmain was always up for some competition.

He was waiting for the right moment to think about the dark horse for it to appear in public with everybody watching.

Benjamin was in the shopping precent there's quite a lot of people and as benjmain was just about to make an appearance as he turns around a corner.

As Benjamin walks up to a group of people a few adults and some children he stops them, asking them for their attention and gets it too as he tries to summoned up the dark horses this time on this occasion does not make it.

The small crowd walks away Benjamin had made himself look like an idiot in and out.

Benjamin was surprised and was not understanding that the dark horse did not turn up and then only then that benjmain realises that his sleeves had gone.

As he tries to clash his arms together he gets an reaction and benjmain walks out of the shopping centre.
Looking stupid and feeling the same way no better than the day before

Benjamin still does not understand he still does not get it that he had been chosen Benjamin wanted to speak to the old Chinese guy.
As Benjamin was thinking hard, he sees him and he shouts loudly to grab his attention. " Hay, wait , you".
The man disappears Benjamin thinks that he is in luck as he follows the man. Once again benjmain is running off in the wrong direction.

Benjamin tries to clash his arms to summon up the dark horse nothing appears or occurs and yet again Benjamin is on his own. The old man could just about be seen in a close distance Benjamin was is closer except the little Chinese man had disappeared.

Once again Benjamin is at a loss and finally gets the idea that he is being mis lead and Benjamin finally begins to think and was thinking that he was not going to choose the little Chinese man.

Benjamin would wait for him which was a good idea to approach him. He was in no know rush in wanting to meet the man that s medicine changed his life and caused Benjamin well literary forced Benjamin to become this person this kind of super hero.

Benjamin was nearly their the old man realises what
Benjamin was now doing and realsies he had lost.

Benjamin had stopped following the old man from the
herbal remedy shop he began to read Benjamins mind.
The following was now the followed.
Benjamin was busy walking back in the opposite
direction speaking to him self asking himself why and
how did this happen to him and other questions that he
thought that he needed to speak about.

Benjamin wanted some answers he thinks that they
need answering.
Why me he continues what's the real reason how did
this happen why me he says again what did I do I
means super powers it s not sane I am no longer sane I
know I am not sane because Benjamin had ran out of
excuses.

Benjamin did not realise that he was being followed by the old Chinese medicine man as he was talking to himself thinking that nobody was listening the medicine man and answering Benjamins questions Benjamin catches on turning around.

As Benjamin bumps straight in to the little medicine man and grabs him Benjamin shouts at him " what did you do to me ".
The medicine man " I thought it would suit you."
Benjamin "What."
Benjamin plees " I am really not cut out for this."
Old man" What."
benjmain" come on you do not think that I do not know what you are, the things that you have done".
Old man" There is an antidote"
Benjamin" Good that makes me feel a lot better."
where is it."
 Old man" Its in China of course".

Benjamin" What do you mean it is in China that's that way".
"Benjamin you are the perfect person by the way. I have to say."

Benjamin turns back around to think the little Chinese medicine man was gone

Benjamin was nearly home and a lot of the questions that Benjamin needed answers for had been answered. Benjamin was not interested in in or about super hero powers all he wanted was the cure so he did not have to be this other person and did not have this side kick that refused to turn up when supposedly being summoned up.

Benjamin had heard everything that the little Chinese man had said and Benjamin was close and was trying to figure him out. As well as himself.

As Benjamin turns the corner at the end of his street he can see the police and they are looking straight at him. Benjamin realises some thing was up and he knew that he could not just turn around.
As he gets closer he finds himself he finds that he feels a bit heavy as his sleeves have appeared

Benjamin is getting closer he is trying to keep himself cool as he needs to pass them, as Benjamin loses his bottle for the first time he could not bring himself to walk past them.

He crosses to the other side of the road only to be called upon the police man wanted him benjmain was under a rest.

Benjamin" Wait I have done nothing" .

Police man " excuse me sir we would just like to ask you a few questions".

Benjamin" What question I have been out of town".

Benjamin is put in to the police car. "Mind your head your detained".

Benjmain said that he could not believe it when they said that he had bad mouth [=ed them and himself as he looked upwards after wards by the two police men in front of the police car.

Benjamin could deal with the sleeves as when he looked upwards and catches the police mans eyes in the rear view mirror asks Benjamin the man what was he looking at and wanted a verbal confrontation the argument begins benjmain shy's away being careful of what he says and then just loses it. Benjmain was wat6chiung the dark horse he was close by.

Benjmain already knew that the dark horse was waiting for him.

CHAPTER 4

Benjamin was hesitating to use his powers his mind was telling him some thing as he was in trouble he was in the police car mind you what are super powers for abusing and using so Benjamin with out another thought and as the sleeves were out and clashes them. The police car is twisted up and over on one side the sleeves were that power full. The dark horse arrives on the scene with the little Chinese medicine man.

The two police officers were ok nobody got hurt benjmain was freed after the chinses man breaks Benjamins hand cuffs off him.

The dark horse disappeared with the medicine man
benjamin was left on his own to make it back home.

Benjamins sleeves disappear again he was just getting
used to this in fact after beating the law he was having a
boast to himself telling himself the story of it all of
what had just happened it was cool benjmain thought it
ws not cool no it was not cool he could not make up his
mind and as excited as he was out at that point he knew
and still he had trouble excepting it.

Benjamin disappears down his road and waits until it
looked safe to approach his apartment.
Benjamin, was in no rush to open the door he was a
little more normal now he had experienced the horse
and now he was waiting for the old ,medicine man to re
appear and tell him what was next.
Benjamin gets in side finally he is in the cold and is in
need of some warming up. He lights a fire quickly and
sets himself up perfectly within a few minutes he would
be warm.

Benjamin looks in his mirror image reflection only for
the fact that he ws looking at his own reflection in his
front room benjmain was looking at the sleeves they
were looking bigger and stood out they looked like
large tattoos running down from his elbow down his
ulnar as he admires them he is thinking that they did not
look to good or look that bad at a second glance.

There's a knock at the door benjmain needs to think about what he is doing he still does not understand he goes off to answer the door knocking then realises that his sleeves are glowing brightly as they light up Benjamin knows that he has company Benjamin takes a step back wards then just as there another knock at the door Benjamin catches on.

Benjamin as nervous as he is begins to talk to himself as he is making an quick escape out of the kitchen window down the escape and back in to the street.

Benjamin is trying to go un noticed and it looked like Benjamin new secret was no longer a secret. Benjamin was not only being watched he was being followed not just by this old Chinese medicine man a horse with the brightest red eyes the feds were on top of that one.

Benjamin finally flips in a shop nearby close to his home he was shouting at people and then started to avoid them it would happen at night making things even harder. And the police were called on a few occasions.

Benjmain was going nuts out of his mind.

On this occasion Benjamin was spot on as he leaves the cops wee just coming in as they pass each other though the shop door entrance bumping shoulders and picking fights as they are nearly caught.

As soon as Benjamin is back out side he runs down street not knowing where he was heading not only this as he comes to the end of his sprint he is summoning things up.
Knowing that he can not go home and the city was a good place to be at that moment and Benjamin needed another place to stay.

Benjamin looks for his wallet in side of his jacket it ws not their he double checks and he is out of luck.
Everything had gone wrong on that particular day Benjamin was questioning his luck as well as his sanity.

Benjamin puts one hand in to his pocket he s got a couple of quid and the beers that he had just brought with the piece of paper.

On this piece of paper was a phone number Benjamin remembers it was Lucy's number Benjamin smiles as he reaches back in to his jacket pocket and finds the coin and it fits in to the phone box that he is standing out side of.

That's a coincidence Benjamin thought. Except for one thing lucy did not pick up and that was the last of Benjamin money his bank cards was still in his wallet and that was just another worry as for some actual money if he wanted some he would have to recover his wallet or go home.

Benjamin funds a door way it is nice and dark and cold which was not so good. Benjamin is naturally getting more worried.

Ass he speaks to himself telling himself and promising himself that he would give himself more time to practice his newly formed powers and with tht he calms down and has a good think of where he should go to practice these new skills these newly formed powers.

Meantime Lucy was having trouble s of her own her car had run out of petrol and she was stuck in the most awkward of places up a mountain. Or I suppose you could call it a tall hill.

Lucy is really wishing that benjmain was there hoping that he would turn up just out of the blue. She was getting upset with her self and the wrong people and with that she was giving people that walked by her weird looks not on purpose however the expression on her face was scaring people.

Lucy was waiting for some help and it was also a busy place for people to walk lucy was busy asking passer byes for petrol, most people ignored her some people just laughed and it was soon realised tht nobody was there to help her.

Benjamin while Lucy was in trouble as more people gathered around her mostly bad people they were listening to her he could hear everything seeing had become extremely good in fact super good.

He knew where Lucy was and he was on hi9s way with the clash of his sleeves on his arms the dark horse arrives.

This time Benjamin is riding the dark horse he is leading the way and when the dark horse stands still as it comes to a holt it speaks to Benjamin as surprised as benjmain is now even more so and Benjamin does not catch on until they had collected lucy.

Benjamin and the dark horse first mission was a success, lucy thinks that she was dreaming Benjamin had no special suit yet however Lucy's compliment that benjmain was still a hunk went down well.

There was no action or violent in benjmain approach as he just whisked her up, On to the dark horse. Afterwards and after Lucy's had thanked Benjamin finally goes home he ahs no other problems. Benjamin was not doing what he is supposed to be doing as he is thinking about it instead whilst he waists time the lesser people who are in danger.

Everybody his sleeves that were built in to him like a tattoo would appear he was off with the dark horse to save them.

CHAPTER 5

However Benjamin wanted more and he puts some of his own ideas of being a super hero to lucy she was already very impressed by how much in that one word had changed things and him from being a hero to being a nothing she had called him.

A nothing she said reminding benjmain about who he used to be.

Benjamin dreams and some of his thoughts are becoming real with the use of his mighty powers Benjamin commits a robbery this would change everything. Lucy knew it was all over the news benjmain did not know and he did not come in he had lost control of himself and it was true he was looking at things from a darker point of view.

Their were darker things a head of him and darker sides of things.
Benjmain had lost control he kept on saying that he would stop but he did not, Lucy approaches him he did not want to see her or speak to her and more then on one occasion had slammed the door in her face.

The darker part of the dark horse had taken over
Benjamins mind in stead of doing good they both had
set their hearts on doing the bad.
Benjamin was spending most of his time in bear in a
strip club drinks where on the house was Benjamin
new saying.
Benjamin was thinking about his appearance he knew
that his new powers had left him bullet proof he could
dodge bullets saving humans only to have nothing in
return but a curse of it and it was a curse of benjmain
actions.

Benjamin was half drunk and leaning on a piece of
paper he was looking straight at it and it had a costume
on it Benjamin looks at it harder. He picks up the piece
of paper not thinking and screws it up. As he throws it
over his shoulder not realising that it was going to be
his costume.

Benjamin realises what he has done he walks off
keeping the picture and his battle armour in mind.
When he had finished speaking to lucy she had not
forgiven him and at this time it's Benjamin on the
receiving end as the door gets slammed in his face.

Benjamin had his fun and with the last mouth full of beer he was thinking about the last few weeks and thinking about the robbing of the post office American, one bank. A fort and a couple of old granny just for fun now he has to go back to business.

Lucy has called upon him and benjmain lets her back in to him Lucy knew a lot and has to say to Benjamin especially about the last couple of months she had the right to know and to know to question him.

Benjamin was not two shy of telling her of the super powers and they both agree for a while it had corrupted him. Lucy was telling benjmain this time around that it was good to have him back.

Benjamin was busy now telling them both why he ahd said the things that he had said he could not get the little old chinses medicine man out of his head benjmain was feed up of the man following him around and being given lessons about the dark horse when Benjamin did not want them.

Benjamin looked like he was going to lose it gain.

Chapter 6

When Benjamin wakes up he wakes up right thinking almost straight away about how he got himself in the upright position the position that he was in.

It looked like Lucy was going to give him a break after misusing his super powers and robbing. Mind you a large quantity was left to the poor so he half good and some thing positive came out of it in the end.
And lots of people were made better off.

Lucy had made the discission for Benjamin and it looked like all the hard work wass not just for himself. When Benjamin agrees Lucy is really pleased happy that some thing good was happening to the both of them through benjamins recent actions. And as she says to him in a joking manor that he should don it again. Benjmain looks at her side ways. " please do not" were benjmain s words.

Lucy" why not you just made that nuns day".

Benjamin" How much is left".

Lucy" I am not sure I was not counting, however the gold is feeling a little heavy".

Benjamin" Who's next"

Lucy" I am not sure".

Benjamin says children's homes Lucy agrees that would be perfect.

Benjamin and lucy move the gold in to her car it was not the easiest thing to do in the middle of the day with the sun blasting down wards on top of you. Around lunch time.

Benjamin still agreed it would have been just as easy or as hard in the night time. at least they did not have to worry who was coming around the corner next to them.

However it just looked like they were moving house. As Lucy comes to the last block s she tells Benjamin that was the last of it. Lucy continued. Meantime Benjamin is busy totally unfocused thinking about his new out fit he had found a nice long coat. That covers Benjamin right from his top to the bottom of his legs. Near his feet it was some thing he could run in it and ride the dark horse in it.

He had required a large half like a large gardening hat it was and looked like an old Chinese fisher mans hat it suited Benjamins style and very soon Benjamin was going to meet that creature that saves him a raven.

Benjamin ahd noticed that the raven was following him he had seen it about Benjamin wanted to meet it.

Benjamin teams were coming together everyday they would meet and discuss and speak in some way together some how. The raven would guard them from above then it would follow it they learnt new things while watching the bird up in the sky's.

The bird was a quick one and it could never be spotted it just seemed to blend in to the sky and the sky's back ground. As for the horse he ahd already been introduced it was now just Lucy.

Lucy was just a normal girl that got on with benjmain from his old college days. How ever she had she had the tendency's of turning up at the right times she was a cool one a cool chick she clearly favoured Benjamin how ever benjmain was to busy to notice.

And so when ever she clicked on to Benjamin was so for himself to understand what lucy was attempting to do often would try and use her conversation to get closer to Benjamin. The subject of the conversation was getting closer.

He prompted away by his new ,master the old Chinese medicine man Benjamin thinks that Lucy was jealous.

Then dark horse team were about to make and become the talk of the town and the city. Lucy wants Benjamin to think an about her and about which area they would be working in Benjamin answer was all of them. Lucy says nothing. The medicine man does not think that he should do to much. His heart was of a good nature.

Benjamin was ready to complain if he was allowed to rob banks and feed the poor what was lucy left to do and what was she supposed to be doing what was Benjamin supposed to be doing. Benjamin blasphemes saying to lucy what the hell does the team want for him to write the bible or save a bunch of two faced nuns, At that point Lucy but in saying to Benjamin as the old man buts in al of them well two of them tell Benjamin to clam down.

Benjamin was getting good as for losing conversations with little lucy it looked like lucy was an intelligent one the old Chinese medicine man was watching them both carefully.

k again
Lucy" So you can talk"

Benjamin " are you serious"
" Yes" Benjamin buts in going off in to one of his
mood s he was clearly misunderstood by this Benjamin
felt nothing as he was over whelmed lucy now
understood him Benjamin was happy he did not know
how to act.

Benjamin was being Benjamin and he also knew that he
owed lucy with his newly formed relationship and his
friends lucy forces an apology even though they said
there was no reason for him to apologise or feel
apologetic as Benjamin agreed as he had know way of
knowing.

Once again benjmain has returned the ,money that he
had stolen all of it, his life seemed to change he could
see the light again I supposed that you could cal it that.

Lucy wanted to talk about it and sounded like Benjamín
he Had a really good time being the bad guys for once
in his life now he battled himself back he re formed
himself form bei9ng bad to being good lucy was
baffled.

Lucy laughs with benjmain as telling him that he
deserved an award for his efforts. Benjmain thinks
about the comment and compliment Benjamin switches
the comment off as they were not so spiritual as such.
Lucy did tend to over speak and as joking things ahd
began to effect there feelings about being super hero s
and it was Lucy's humour which was letting her down
benjmain tells her that he actually felt offended .

Lucy could not believe it that her comments which
were not offensive had upset Benjamin lucy could not
believe it as she too now loses her temper the argument
started with her saying what what do you mean/ ah
come on Benjamin you have something to say your
joking right "
Benjamin tells her straight that one joke was enough
she did not have to make a joke in every other sentence.

Benjmains complaint continued and as much as lucy
wanted to say she was well unimpressed and was on the
verge of walking out it was only her humour that kept
her in the argument.

And in the same building as Benjamin in the end some
how Benjamin manages to keep him self in the
conversation that he was sorry about what he had said..
Lucy calls it Benjamin agrees ok lucy says quite them
ok Benjamín reply's ill quite them they had agreed and
Benjamin was right bck in business he was getting it
right again his sleeves light up again and Benjamin and
the dark horse were back in business, the dark horses
was awaiting just out side.

Benjamin mounts the dark horse it was obvious to
Benjamin and the stallion horse super fast red eyes that
kind of thing and it spoke.
Benjamin start the conversation the horses mind
worked like a radio it just knew things that you would
not know.

He tells Benjamin what his problem was where the problem was and it would take Benjamin their.

As they reach the target it looked like Benjamin team had got there in second place the [police had got their before them once again benjmain needs to keep his cool there was a lot of people around him he did not want to scare people. In fact he was doing the opposite in fact he needed them. The

Chapter 7

more people that he met with the dark horse the more popular he thought he would feel the more comfortable his team would feel.

Benjamin has a jumper the horse is the first to speak, Benjamin understands him he has to go upstairs to convince the client that he had a choice and that he did not have to jump.

Once again Benjamin had introduce himself as the dark horse to the authority's and to the police, he tells the client that he was safe and that he could trust him and he should hand himself over.

The police agree also and it was said and agreed by Benjamin sleeve. Benjamin is talking to him and he s agreeing that the jumper could take a lot of pressure off hem both if he would step away. He asks the jumper if he wanted to talk a stupid question but has to be asked.

The police were asking Benjamin the same question he could be brought down stairs from up their.

The dark horse team were up for the job and benjmain was going back up stairs to the roof of the building to the top of the office building.

The man was clearly insane and seriously dangerous and problem off his face and believed that he was r4eady to die. What ever had told him this was even had more of a problem.

While Benjamin was talking to the man he finds out that it was no joke the man the jumper was serious. Benjamin who was taking the whole thing lightly as his talking did not help and was not working it was typical science a typical scene. The jumper was in the paper already the article read dark horse fails again it was all over the press the next morning.

And just to make things worse even more complicated they had more press right out side their door this was going to be an on going thing benjmain thinks.

Benjmain could see Lucy's point and lucy tells Benjamin that he better think quickly h=and have some thing to say to them

As regards to the police turning up also outs ide of Benjamins apartments.

They did not put the blame fully on Benjamin however he was the person who was supposed to in control Lucy said the word prison and Benjamin could not believe it he continued down town in there offices he has nothing to hide and she told them the truth how could he lie he said.

He as an audience and everybody knew that he was the good guy. This sounded a little bit cocky but it was true. He had been gifted.

Benjamin still denied the changes they were changed as the press had full coverage Benjamin was on TV.

As for the man on the ledge he had jumped he fell with Benjamin as they both plumet to the ground over the edge only for Benjamin to break his fall except as he braces himself Benjamin feels his sleeves power up they were not saved yet and benjmain was expecting a visitor. The man who looked like he was going to die was not saved as he lied dead in Benjamins arms his body disappears in to pure light.

Before the man disappears all Benjamin could do was to cradle the man. Until the right authority's arrive Benjamin was taken by his arms.

Everything was quiet at Benjamins home nobody would speak until lucy finally breaks the ice, slowly at Benjamin telling him it was not his fault and that he had been given permission to do what he had done he had permission to approach the man.

It was needed Benjamin knocks it off as Benjamin was slowly signs of remorse and lucy was not buying it.

Lucy gets the idea that something else was going on Benjamin was not just feeling guilty he was nothing it was his newly formed partner ship with his newly formed powers the super powers. He did not want to be the dark horse.
Lucy had now agreed to agree that benjmain was now totally nuts. Benjamin was looking straight at Lucy. "What".

Benjamin reply's nothing. Benjamin then speaks." It was not my fault" Lucy tells Benjamin that he had finally caught on she continued finally you dope it was not your fault.
Benjamin had agreed and it was another long conversation started however Benjamin was willing to talk about it.

A week passes and Benjamin is doing more than the police they did not kind the press where now constantly following Benjamin for his efforts it was not that bad. The horse the bird and Lucy with Benjamin and the old man were all getting good.

It was the bad guys turn to do some damage to Benjamin's city lucy had already been kidnapped a couple of times each time Benjamin and the dark horse would come to the rescue. However on this occasion Benjamin fails and the dark horse try's to follow through but he fails also.

It was only the old Chinese medicine man who was left with his raven. This was put to Benjamin by the bad guys who now had Lucy and Benjamin tired up attached to some TNT. That's dynamite .
With both of them tied up they were not in the position of being in a life saving conversation which would always work.

Benjamin and Lucy we were counting on the raven to help them who was counting on the old medicine man with the raven extremely close by on his shoulder and with the old man making an approach his captive friends where in a hard position right in the centre of the city.

The old medicine man needs an excuse and he is
willing to make an approach he claimed that he did not
like things like that however he turns himself invisible
and disappears as he stands next to the Benjamin
asking him if he could see him as Benjamin says yes
the old man denies it and claims that Benjamin could
not see him even though Benjamin could see him the
old man was making games.

The raven too thinks Benjamins was nuts that he had
lost it and agrees that he too know could not be seen
benjmain is thinking that they are thinking funny. There
was a man was going to make an approach he would
disguise himself as himself the old medicine man he
would pretend that he had lost the girl. And get in
so=side of Benjamins mind.

Lucy's capture s and sees them by controlling the bad guys minds it would be great idea and as the old medicine ma manages to pull it off.

Invisibility was the old mans secret benjmain was looking straight at lucy who was looking straight back lucy muffled words some thing along the lines of I do not want to die benjmain needed her to understand that he was in the same position.

He whisper s to lucy through his gag that was as loud as he could speak. Do not worry we will escape can you feel my sleeves they are on their way to us.

Benjamin was using his eyes he could see everything his capturers were trying to calm Lucy down telling to shut up and telling her she should listen because she was going to die. This did not help Lucy who was busy talking back to Benjamin this did not help their or Benjamins or even Lucy's situation. Lucy was busy speaking and once again she was invited to shut her mouth. Lucy was wishing it her self but she just continued talking lucy knew that she was really screwed and she was the one who was now cracking up.

This was a new experience for Lucy she looked now stronger than Benjamin except on this occasion she was faking it out Benjamin could see why. It was the TNT. That was extremely upsetting her it was on the floor right in front of them. It was moving about ticking and as the more that they worried about it the more that it seemed to move around.

There was a scorpion on top of it moving with its vibration. It eventually got board of the TNT and was now heading over in their directions before Lucy could scream it was crawling up on to her.
This was scary. Lucy could feel it. And she could see it as it crawls up her thigh in to her lap. Benjamin is upset of course he could not help her his sleeves were nearly ready it was just a matter of time Lucy was trying to scream however her mask prevented her.

Benjamin once he was free thought for a while
believing that it was a joke a bad joke a sick one in fact
lucy agreed. As she nods and seems to speak in saying
ohooch as Benjamin removes the tape from across her
mouth.

The old man the bird and the horse had found
Benjamin and Lucy and within the hour there capturers
had fled and they are all on the news again they were on
there way.

Benjamin would hear the word they sounded ferocious
and up in the clouds the sky above them it looked storm
full. Benjamin could tell it was going to be one of
those nights.
Once they had discussed that couple days of adventure
everybody was in good then of adventure everybody
was good where the raven Benjamin says as he had not
yet made an appearance. The raven was missing
however as Benjamin was just about to question it
again the raven swoops in side through right through
Benjamins apartment window and then returns in to the
opposite direction and lands straight on the old
medicine s mans shoulder. It says nothing however
Benjamin gets the ideas that it was smiling.

Benjamin could believe it as the raven makes a perfect landing and starts to speak the raven spoke. Ok Lucy says staring right at Benjamin and then the bird. In disbelief and as the old man sniff at another pork ball in to his mouth saying while eating and speaking with his mouth full tells the raven that it was a classy thing to do. Nobody knew what they were talking about.

The raven picks at a pork ball.

Lucy too wanted to eat but the old man knew an d pushes the plate of food towards her she is grateful with a smile on his face. The old man lucy explains to Benjamin was always willing to share. . It was a good feeling Lucy says in return.
Lucy" It is not about the way I feel it's the way I feel about you".

Benjamin interrupt's and is asking her if that was some kind of verse from a book as he says that he had read it some where he says that he had heard it before.

The old Chinese medicine man says that he was just making it up, Benjamin looked like a fool for the first time. in fact he ten continued that he read off an news paper this made Benjamin look like an even bigger fool. Lucy did not find his second attempt to hurt Benjamin as funny as the first time and they put it down to the old mans humour.
Benjamin was a little surprised.

Chapter 8

They both agree that the old man made a meal of it neither of them would enjoy the Chinese food and Benjamins was off like a shot down town to some good old fashioned stuff. Just to get his own back and put the old man to shame, which he does.
Benjamin was feeling a little bit more like himself Lucy was quick to his side lucy was talking to him about what an adventure she was having

Benjamin was having enough already are you crazy he thought you have just been freed from a box of TNT.

Lucy" Yeah" lucy says smiling

Benjamin" Your nuts totally nuts"

Lucy smiles Benjamin she says saying nothing what ever it is Benjamin has no idea of what she was trying to say.

Benjamin smiles in side of the shop ah he says junk food he says oh yes you can have anything you like.

Lucy "Good at least that's a reply."

Benjamin" why" benjmain ahd to ask.

Lucy" meet me half way I agree to all of your terms and not only this I have drawn up a contract for me to you meet me I am your new side kick."

"erh"

Benjamin says before you say no it is to late you did say anything. Benjamin is in shock and he found it quite funny and congratulates her in her newly formed

position. Benjamín says yes Lucy says that she was his girl.
She says to benjmain that she was ready to be his side kick so she continued this time she was asking for some super powers her question was now where were hers .

Benjamin does not know do not ask me he says and then an ahhh and an uuuh and then he speaks that is you.
I am afraid little lucy side kick of the dark horse or some thing there is no more unfortunately and fortunately benjmain has already been chosen..
That's exactly what I have been trying to say for the last hour.
There can only be one dark horse lucy says to them both that it was a little disappointing. They both agree. Lucy brushes it off. haying she said that the costume was enough anyway.

Benjamín turns around noticing the suit that lucy was now called to remove by the old medicine man the suit was a costume as lucy changes she tells them why she was wearing it she said that she just wanted to play the part.

That good Lucy however like a medicine man says that there can be only one dark horse and it is me.
Lucy just looks at him and then walks outside telling them both that she will be out side waiting do not forget the peanuts that was the last thing she had said. When they came out of the shop Lucy was not their she ws just over the road fighting crime yelling at some tramp for speaking to her impolite about Benjamin and the dark horse and to top it all off.

To round things off her missing suit was returned to her as a safety measure it was topic of conversation as the subject had been brought up twice now in conversation. She said that she was now making progression. She says.

Benjamin has no choice but to stop Lucy she thinks she is doing good as Benjamn has to pull her off the tramp.

In fact it was not the old man it was a younger man Benjamin has to tell the police man who tells Benjamin that the description was a wrong as he turns to question Lucy again about the eyes of the man that she says that he was trying to used Benjamin super powers laughing

After they had got their story straight the officer lets them go.
And on that occasion Benjamin and lucy had to laugh, as for what Lucy had done. The very next morning both of them were at the breakfast table. The raven appears ;landing perfectly on Benjamin's shoulder the right one as his left one was facing the bright sunshine.
Benjamin receives the message and the raven leave s him again not to far on lucy and Benjamin are watching it fly. As it circles around.

That was weird lucy ahd thought Benjamin says yes he agrees and tells her that it was a little more than weird, as for demonic horses with bright red eyes birds that can talk and old chinse medicine men please lucy try to explain it to me again.

Because I can not deal with this I cannot make heads or tails of the whole thing it is driving me nutty.
Lucy's replied was one of a surprise totally cool she says that's the spirit Benjamin totally cool.

The next time the raven lands to speak to them it land s on Benjamin's shoulder to speak to Lucy it spoke gently and greatly to explain to Lucy telling her that while he was up there above them he had heard every word.

Lucy shy's away your good really good lucy says no more as she hangs her head in shame even though the bird was right lucy was backing her self up. She says it in a weird voice which took benjmain by surprise as he was right in front of her listening I was talking about you not too you.
Benjamin smiles and lucy says to the raven that she was sorry she did not mean to offend him.

I thought that we were team mates friend I was just making fun you know jokes. Lucy was bring one on as she continued her explanations were going to take all day for the length of her apology to the raven went on over five minutes now benjmain was really smiling as Lucy continued to lay it on.

Lucy was really laying it on, knowing that the raven was going to catch on, only a week later realises what was good.

Lucy and Benjamin are in fits of laughter when out of nowhere the raven which was usually flying about them was normally above them fly's back in side as it lands on benjmain shoulder to tell them that he excepts their apology but lucy was now clearly allergic of the bird.

Or she was just pretending acting funny about benjmain having another side kick. Lucy was jealous.

Benjamin wanted to know the truth.

What had lucy done to be arrested by the police again and why did she want to be a super hero could she not see that what Benjamin was going through was a curse, a big one. One that will never leave them. One that will stick to your life but one that will change you greed. Selfishness, and will probably kill you. Or get you killed.

However ready you are or know that the hero always wins.

Lucy was really laying it on knowing that the raven was not going to catch on only a week later realises what lucy had now said.

Lucy and Benjamin are in fits of laughter when the raven returns out of no where which was unusual for it flying about them around them and above them as it fly's around in circles then lands upon not Benjamin's shoulder buts lucy's. Lucy was allergic of the bird.

Or she was just being funny about Benjamin having another side kick, Benjamin wanted to know the truth.

What had they done to get herself in that position, Lucy had been arrested and why did she want to be a super hero. Could she not see that what they were talking about was a curse a big one, that would never leave you. One that would suck the life form you and it will change you greedy, selfish and probably kill you in the end. However you all ready knew that the hero always wins.

Chapter 9

The raven pecked Lucy o0n her cheek gently lucy and caught on.
Benjamin too had caught on the raven before any of them get a chance to speak to it again for a while. Lucy and Benjamin says it was a compliment lucy was surprised that the raven gave her an apology lucy gets all flustered her face turned bright red.

Lucy with the embarrassment and in shock is chocking in each sentence as she tries to speak and in the end errh

I hate him just wait. She continued with the waving of her fist to it as it fly's by them outside by Benjamins window cill.

Benjamin who had required super hearing was listening to the outside s there ws no signs of danger yet.
The raven could hear them all and it knew it was Benjamin and he knew that he needed to get his back.
Meantime lucy was looking at the old Chinese medicine man it was unusual for him not to make an appearance to them.

Lucy after a good hour of searching for him finally she gives in and goes all the way back upstairs on to the roof and waits for benjmain to make an appearance and for the raven to return.

Benjamin was busy trying to figure out his powers while the raven returns keeping watch while Benjamin talks to the dark horse.
It looked like the lucy had or was missing out she was struck out while everybody else was at play. Lucy chooses to pretend to play pretending to a super hero. Not realising that there was a super villain right behind her when lucy turns around she knew what she was she was greeting and she shouts as loud s she could.
Benjamín becomes dark horse.

Lucy is in trouble busy being kidnapped as she try's to threaten her captors she did not recognise them this time around. As lucy complains get off I've got super powers did you not know. And get of me you thug these were lucy words as she fights them off her verbally.

Benjamin could near the whole thing he was close by and while lucy is trying to get them to give her what they wanted un aware of which street gang she was speaking to. Once lucy is back in her chair she is questioned on the subject super powers they seemed to think that lucy in her costume not an suit had the super powers that Benjamin yielded.

Look mister lucy says which a big smile on her face who ever you are I am not the dark horse the men questioning her did not believe her and made her agree that she was to the point of convincing lucy who had been seen the dark horse.
Lucy was far from convincing however she manages to tell the bad guys still that she has no super powers they still again after questioning her did not believe her.

Lucy was running out of ideas she is trapped whilst pretending to be the dark horse side kick which she was once again her captures asked her slowly about her so called super powers the super powers that only Benjamin yielded lucy is realising that the bad guys were now realising that the people in front of her were getting more serious.

Chapter 10

It was clear to Benjamin that the raven had taken the lead in looking for lucy as by being next to Benjamin's side and was following lucy captures knowing that he would find them and turn and take himself back to Benjamin shoulder.

Benjamin so far had mastered his powers his magical chef they looked all electrical and their electric components could be seen clearly as they moved up and down like they had a mind of there own like they were in control of themselves Benjamin had not noticed this before.

Benjamin hears lucy again she was close by just as the raven turns up landing again on Benjamin shoulder and confusing him a little raven Benjamin already n[knew. Yes Benjamin ahd said I have heard its already Lucy's got issues and she's close by and in trouble we should move quickly. She is going ton kick off in a few minutes it so typical of lucy I bet she's just waiting for the chance.

Raven "Ok righty the raven says"

Raven "Do you have her address" .
Benjamin "No need she s close by I can feel her.

The raven takes up in to sky and Benjamin stands up.

Benjamin could feel the power of the dark horse as his
chefs are pulled together once they meet there's a clash
of thunder and the dark horse was summoned. As the
power of the both of them emerged as the power of
them travels through each other a large flash appears
lightening striking him then the dark horse appears the
black stallion with the demonic red eyes and that the
horse in front of Benjamin with the raven on Benjamins
shoulder appears.

Benjamin next move half helped by Raven as they
speedy head of to Lucy's rescue Benjamin is told that
his name was something like the rain master to that is
not it's close the rain says it s hold on I am not the
horse, the raven is puzzled Benjamin as he says like this
no hold on to the dark horse and hold on as I am trying
recollect the bad guys name it was the lightening
Benjamin cuts in while racing up off the darkness with
the dark horse shad ow which was on fire as the dark
horse breathes the flames that also his shadows shadow
finally the raven tells benjmain Lucy's captures name
its ok it's the lightening wizards flew I said it is the
lightening wizard and he's the old wear house.

Benjamin shouts to the raven that they had taken the
wrong route and she was at the old wear house hay the
horses breaths faster dark horse faster Benjamin calls
Lucy we are on our way.

As the dark horse breathes fire through its nose
Benjamin not use to being on horse back is hanging on
for his life. He was getting good but need to learn a bit.

Benjamins horse gets faster as Benjamin holding the Raines with a little attitude tighter however he was just getting used to his new toy and was enjoying himself as for the ride the horse was no different and was no longer running on the ground he was running on the air he was running above the ground its power was of one they called it tremendous mess as its huffs were to enflamed with the power of fire.

As he was leaving tracks of fire behind them as an reminder of their presents nobody dared to follow then yet. They soon disappeared in to the darkness. Benjamins long over coat was also on fire however

Benjamin does not burn and the raven is no fool he is quick to leave Benjamins side on this ride he is quick to leave Benjamin shoulder.

The evening erns the name they called it the evening of raven of fire, the raven leads the way to Lucy s whereabouts Benjamin and the dark horse crashes right through the brick walls that Lucy was kept behind no messing about and straight to the point. Why knock when there a dark horse Benjamin wrote that one down so he would never forget.

Benjamin had noticed that his body had changed he looked like her was perfect he had gone to perfect muscular. And even Lucy had said trim. Which explains why he ws still breaking things as he went by things he put this down to being clumsy. Such things as door handles, twice at te market stalls and tea cups as well as a few other things in Lucy's kitchen also he had changed his hands had grown bigger and he could grip things tightly he could feel the power of his hands.

The only item that he did not break through his powers was the Raines of the Darkhorse they spent most of their time on fire.

As Benjamin steps in to the empty wear house and makes an attempt on saving her he makes it look easy. But only because there was nobody there picks up lucy in his arms as she fainted Benjamin pulls her up half catching her before she hits the floor ss Benjamin picks her up placing her on to the dark horse and sending it away. Leaving the dark horse to do it all over again as its hoof s set on fire setting fore to the room which was empty but still worth bring down.

Benjamin with the Darkhorse lucy and the raven disappear just as the police turn up for the bad guys lucy s kidnappers. Benjamin was looking over his shoulder thinking about the action tat he was missing. Late again but still they came late again as always however Benjamin never actually called the authority to put the flames out that's about as much action that the police had.

Once lucy, Benjamin, Darkhorse the raven and the medicine man had all recovered lucy gives Benjamin an apology Benjamin smiles all in a days work he says boastfully.

Benjmain is looking confused he really needs to practice and explore that he ws on his way to China. When lucy hears of this she jumped at that chance to travel with benjmain however Benjamin had other plans and lucy thinks that she has been left out.

China she says that really great I have always wanted to go there lucy smiles leaning up on to benjmain like girlfriend would do.

You know that the old chinses medicine man would like to take that flight your thinking of taking with you. That's great news benjmain.

Before Benjamin gets the chance to speak lucy had decided that she was being welcomed on a holiday. Benjmain did not have the heart to tell her that he wanted to go on his own and he knew that it would upset everybody but Benjamin is saying that's was his own mission however it was also one of lucy s dreams. In the end after a good long convincing he agrees that they all could do with a break.

After a quick -plane journey and a week of full
intensive and spiritual training of the chefs and the dark
horse China could not of been a better place Benjamin
returns back with lucy and the old medicine man and
the raven who flew most of his journey by himself their
and back faster than Benjamin actual plane.

Once back on federal ground Lucy's appearance was
one to question as she is stopped and searched at the air
port terminal and just to rub ity in again as she
approaches another terminal she is stopped again and is
searched again.
Lucy had not realised that the suit was with a blow up
cushion was a bit over the top as they were coming
back form chia and not Jamaica her dress was not to
impressive and her dress gave her away although she
had not changed. But had gone on past through the
airport hardly unnoticed.

As soon as Benjamin arrives back home trouble starts it is as if it had been waiting there to re arrive trouble starts again Benjamin takes off his disguise as lucy and himself were wearing one glasses and baseball caps.

Lucy is already prepared and now makes sense as for the old man he gets away with it as for his age who would think. The raven was or should of arrived which he did just after Benjamin plane.
He was waiting out side by a taxi for them.

They were al tired from all of the sun and fun in fact Benjamin was so knacked out he tried to run simply because of the dark horse and not ready to ex-plain himself again decides to run with slowly the authorities his passport to be phased and arrested. Only to wake up in a jail the very next morning.

Lucy is well prepared as the raven is as they enter the police station acting like Benjmains manager her total acts starts with hay di you have a man in here. The jailer asks her that would be who?
Come on Mr dark horse of course. I mean benjmain.
Benjamin says polity did you know that the moon is out this v=evening
No I did not.
This converstion was all in code they were speaking about something l=else with what they were saying.
Ok where is he.

I know that he was in here. Benjmain catches on he is being cool behi9nd the bars he could clearly see that it was Lucy and she was enjoying every bit of her time inf front of him as she continues to pretend to be Benjamin lawer as she keeps the guard talking the raven slips I side giving benjmain the keys to the jail. There were some seriously weird people about benjmain as the r even slips him the keys benjmain being as kind as he was lets the rest of the prisoners' out as well as himself.

Benjmain had escaped. The very next morning it was in the news new super hero skips n]=bail fees prisoner's and some other stuff lucy stole the show it looked like a perfect scene.

For the next few days lucy was laughing and benjmain could not believe that she had got her wish to be in fact in the lead.

Well there you go lucy it looks like you are a super hero after all benjmain smiling says those words to her.

Right lucy replies you finally have me down as a super hero

Erh not exactly side kick I prefer.

Right benjmain talking about down to be a super hero I have one more gift for you

Go Lucy's says

I am going back home benjmain has my address do not forget to give it to her. Benjmain the old man continues take this coat wear it when you are in danger and look at it closely it will look like a real jacket however in battle it will become veery powerful like lucy your best friend. It will protect you both super powers are becoming enforced you will not eb or act like anybody else use these gifts wisely. Was the old Chinese medicines man words.

Chapter 11

Benjamin wanted to but in but also he wanted out. It was not for the fact for having the super powers and with all the controversy that came with it. It was a reasonable crazy curse that ws put upon Benjamin of being a super hero.

It was clear to Benjamin it was clear to benjmain and the press that Benjamin had a problem with it. Which was leading him to another problems i9naafact it was benjmain and when benjmain looked gain at it polity the statement that he ahd made and said cheerfully it was the fact that he was actually screwed.

As Benjamin's finds himself on the front page of every news paper it had read as below Benjamin says that he is screwed another paper said that Benjamin was screwed except it was written in reverse so nobody fully understood it.

Lucy on the other side was smooth with compliments you would think for a side kick she was doing good Benjamin would not notice her and he did not care.

For that period Benjamin was not there it took a few good days to get over it to snap out of it and get his head around the rest of the articles and find himself again. Benjamin and all the super hero stuff once he had woken up things were looking good again.

The old man disappears as the raven approaches landing on Benjamin shoulder and sparking loudly there was no message.

Benjamin was in two frames of mind not knowing weather to shout with joy or shout because he was angry with everything that had happened or what was happening lucy could feel it as she approached the old man

Wishing that he would stay Benjamin was to surprised as for when the old man decided just to up and leave. He left them with out any signs or warnings Lucy is watching as the old mans shadow disappears behind the sunset in the distance. Benjamin still is in shock not understanding of why the old man had just upped and left both of there sides the raven did not understand either.

That very evening Benjamin and lucy were having a long conversation about the things that's had happened and start to argue. This was all about the old man about h0ow selfish Lucy believed him to be and about Benjamin thoughts of his aptitude to just up and go.

Benjamin was not aware he was leading himself straight in to trouble benjmain closes his eyes his raven was close by flying around him and landing right on his shoulders Benjamin called it through the power of thought.

Benjamin was getting good at this time he sends for the raven bird again after he had returned he had called it back it had worked Benjamin say s it does and does it again sending the raven away and calling it back the bird was none the less teased in fact he was enjoying it.

Benjamin thinks it is cool he ws having a bit of fun he is delighted with his newly reformed relationship with the raven.

Although Benjamin being and controlling him with his newly found super powers his chefs and dark horse powers are summoned.

And within that call summoned up the raven all together.
The dark horses power was its presents a frightening one it's simple red eyes its stealth and speed in its mood it ran with external powers the dark horse was the first and again benjmain once in control once again benjmain is in control only for a casual approach in his mind.

Benjamins powers were now that he had chosen he was the first page he was the one that was in control of not just Lucy but the bird as well as the old man. All four of them.

Lucy was not to fear to behind him and Benjamin could except her as part of the team. Just his presents next to Benjamin was a power in its self Benjamin was in control.

As benjmain thinks about his powers which he called his gifts as he brings his team together with closed eyes. First to race to his shoulders either side he says to the fresh black bird the silhouette that's sits upon his shoulders them lucy his side kick calls dark horse himself who is unexplained and with them.

Benjamin still does not get the understanding of the dark horse he wants control and the horse is frightening it needed to be tamed. Benjamin needed to understand it, all of it. From the very beginning.

However as a conversation starts one that benjmain one that he would never forget first his eyes then his heart then his ears and then his lungs all filled with fire love and darkness peace all at the same time.

The dark horse appears then Lucy the raven and Benjamin himself a partner ship w=had occurred they were fantastic they were the dark horse.

Once lucy and Benjamin were there on top of there newly required powers they were close by and close by

Benjamins apartment on its roof practicing as lucy watches Benjamin summands the dark horse.

Out of nothing the horse appears after Benjamin clashes his chef together with one sound of thunder and then a flash of lightening the dark horses appears. And then with the opening of the sky close to the ground the dark horse appears with ankles of fire and a burning light and full of electricity his large red eyes the horse was being tamed ass it arises to Benjamin command s. lucy re appears.

The horse rises uo on to the dark black side legs as the lightening hits its surroundings as Benjamins jacket appears and the raven lands down upon Benjamins shoulders.

Benjamin is really impressed with all of them a medical medicine form the chinses man medicine man Benjamin says to himself as lucy nudges him telling himself as he nudges him telling him that he had done good.

The horses approaches Benjamin for the past for a pat on his back and a small cuddle the raven flies off and lucy ws looking for some attention.

The Darkhorse had arisen Benjamin was getting good and he was getting good and summoning and controlling the whole thing in theory lucy said that he was good.

Lucy was in the coat and is trying to figure it out an accident weaponed a Chinese accent story which was true to this day. The coat of flames is now the focus of everybody it could do things to you and them un do them who dared to wear it it could change your thoughts enter your thoughts and tamed your mind. It too wanted to control the dark horse. In fact they were two powers set aside.

Lucy was good the coat of flames worked for her because she thought they were cool and were pure she was kind and it worked as she was thinking good thoughts.

Lucy was good and in sense was in as Benjamin as she is mastering the power of her gift as they battle against each other each other gaining knowledge and shares his secret of there newly formed weapon's.
Infarct lucy got good and the raven landed on her shoulder instead of Benjamin .

Lucy makes a call calling upon her mighty powers the coat of flames using the power of fire to do things like to removes things to do things to cleanse the unjust worthy in fact this so called coat was cool lucy thought it could change a few people s mind about her lucy could change the shape of fire she could use it as a shield of fire. It could protect her an it would form a small shield.

When Benjamin saw this he was seriously impressed as for lucy she was stuck as she calls off her powers only to have a boast straight afterwards benjmain was shaking his head telling her to watch him Benjamin closes his chefs together the power of lightening and thunder would erupted and a massive storm was arisen however the storm a was not just any storm it was not just everywhere and it had come about h=them in as a pair in the form of lightening and then of thunder.

As Benjamin softly watches her saying to himself how powerful he was as Lucy steps backwards until she kneels and uses he super powers to form a shield of fire to protect her from Benjamin super powers of the fire and lightening.

All l it thinks they think that they wee getting to aggressive there attitude was all wrong when lucy bows out
The Raven conversation begins about how powerful the dark horse was. And how powerful the dark horse together were actually extremely powerful.

Benjamin leaves Lucy with the upper hand and knew that the very first battle was her victory Benjamin refused to believe it and was soft as Benjamin well agrees and lucy knows that in there and knows that in there next training battle he would try again he would try and get his unpack.

For once Benjamin as the upper hand but he is slowly losing his mind the contents thought of losing the girl really threatened his position he did not realise that she ws that good. Benjamin is on his knees thinking about the loot his very first time training lesson to his side kick. It was like losing a boxing match in the first round in the first minute.

Lucy had a good reason to boast about her challenge to . Benjamin refuses to talk lucy knew already he was imbraestt however he was running out of the conversation and idea of how to avoid Lucy who wanted to   him about it.

CHAPTER 12

The very next day lucy is awoken with a large smile on her face she was still dreaming of a having her breakfast made then she wakes up right.

Benjamin was standing up near her as she wakes with a smile and a yawn. Benjamín hands her a cue of coffee and as she awakes she wanted to go straight outside outrates and train why lucy knew why however she was not decided when she should do battle she wakes quickly ups stairs upon the roof.

The battle of her powers begin lucy gets it right benjmain gets in the way. As lucy makes some more moves towards benjmain shouting out at her while protecting himself that benjmain as the battle of powers begin as lucy protects her self she had improved benjmain should think about his heart this where his power lays
You need to think Lucy says lucy to her self out loud. As she dodges one lightening bolt t=and then the sound of thunder.

Benjamin still trying hard lucy notices and attempts to help Benjamin he retaliates verbally blocking her attack with his arms and striking her with a bolt of electric.

Knocking her back a few steps and shouting again at her as she welcomes him some more only to discourage e her as he strikes her again.

Shouting again this time straight from his heart he shouts benjmain had formed the darkness of love. Lucy had helped Benjamin as Benjamin is understanding himself and his powers that he called the dark horse. As he lays this words not realising that just one sentence would summoned the dark horse it was not the chefs at all. Another lesson about his mighty mistico's powers was learnt.

Lucy is now being left behind and Benjamin and the dark horse are quickly winning each other back. Lucy looked like she needed a rest Benjamin calls out toner as he bonds with the dark horse the horse looked at lucy his eye bright red.

It was true Benjamin says I have nothing left you win the raven
Nicely put Benjamin do not mind if I do. The raven understand s him and fly's over to Lucy's and sits perched on higher shoulder Lucy and Benjamin find out some thing ne the raven takes sides.

The very next morning Lucy awakes with a big smile on her face she was dreaming of having her breakfast made and brought up to her. Then she wakes up. Benjamin was standing close by to her. As she fully awakes with a smile and a yawn. Benjamin hands her a cup of coffee and as she awakes again Benjamin wants to train lucy knew why however she was not deterred as for a challenge from benjmain and hoses battle over peace as she prepares her self quickly they meet up stairs on the roof top.

Their battles of powers begin Lucy's gets right up close to Benjamin as he pushes her off him in a return. Lucy gets it right Benjamin gets in lucy s way. As lucy makes an other move on Benjamin, Benjamin is quick to answer her. As he breaks form her hold and moves away form her only to move back in to her closer.

Lucy catches on she was not tat bad and was thinking quickly as she now was protecting her self. Benjamin was thinking about his heart that's where his power was. You need to think lucy says ducking and moving around a lightening bolt.

Benjamin is trying to hard and Lucy notices ands offers
to help him he retaliates verbally blocking Lucy's
attack with his arms and then striking her with
lightening one bolt of electricity.

Knocking her back wards not once but twice. As she
shouts at him as he welco0mes her more only to move
right he strikes her again. As he shouts at her again a
battle cry. Shouting again Benjamin had moved
forwards out of the darkness of love.

Lucy had helped Benjamin in a big way Benjamin was
still understanding his powers that they called dark
horse.
As he says those words not realising that he would
summoned up the creature another lesson was learnt.
Lucy was busy being left behind. And Benjamins
quickly winning his battle back. He tells Lucy as sure
as he was that she needed a break a rest. Benjamin calls

out to her this time it was him that was giving her the advice, and not the other away around.

The dark horse was standing there moving his feet as if to say I not only a horse but I am power full. As he rubs his hoof on the dusty floor of the roof top. His eyes half red and glowing.

Its time Benjamin I have noth8ng left for you it was the raven it had found them again I have to say it was nicely put the raven understands lucy and Benjamin found out some thing new the raven was taking up sides.

It looked like Lucy had put benjmain on his arse for the first and last time as they both were gaining understanding of there newly inherited powers benjmain was going to have a boast and as for lucy she could see an argument arising as for the fact that benjmain wass just a little bit byv far powerful than her. Benjmain did not realise that he had hurt her not lucy once in battle but verbally too. With the powers of his conversation.

Lucy takes the last strike and Benjamin calls it a day.

This time around Benjamin is doing the dreaming as he to now is sitting down on the roof watching the dark horse and while thinking of his master the old Chinese medicine man.

Benjamin is confused about what he was suppose to do now to be what he was doing he was in general still upset about having to figure it all out by himself. With very little guidance. And having to deal with lucy on top of everything else.

Benjamin insists if he had been listening that comes
back of course lucy was saying to the rian that begins
that is insane and he would have been up on the roof
talking to their master.
The raven looked down upon lucy as lucy looks up at
the raven the raven shouts squeaks kind of chirps a cry
of war. As lucy shouts at Benjamin

The date was the twenty's eighth it was Benjamin s
birthday Benjamins celebration had been missing form
him since he was a child since Benjamin a was very
young.

Benjamin was a good child however his parents thought differently as well as his brothers who have past away. As for his aptitude and when he told himself that he did not time he had left his family's side.

Benjamin had escaped them by leaving via his bedroom window down a tree and onto the street where he stayed for a few years until he had found another home and got his life back in the order that it should have been in.

He made it easy for himself making that decision   and had done his self a favour after a few months being in the cold Benjamin was up and back on his feet.

Benjamin awakes roughly he had fallen asleep getting up sleep asking makes his way down stairs while talking to himself, straight past Lucy who was in the kitchen.
Lucy does not interfere as Benjamin looks like crap and she knew not to speak to him she had heard rumours of this experience as it was Benjamins state pf mind she had been told and slaps Benjamin around this face not once but twice to wake him. To wake him from his wake to wake him up.

Benjamin catches on lucy attempt had failed as for the second time and attempt as she holds on tightly what they had was enough.

Benjamin lets go of her hand lucy says sorry apogees Benjamin tells her it did not matter Lucy's guess that Benjamin was on a mad one a bad dream or some thing along those lines either lucy was keeping her problems to her self lucy ws the only person who knew but this was not going to help as she pretended to understand which mad there problems worse it would be a lie.

Lucy new that she had made the right discission to leave Benjamins to Benjamin.
He had woken up, however he was confused about how he got in to the kitchen from the roof up stairs bringing back the smiles that was usually on his face. As lucy has to explain that he had walked benjmain does not believe it as he does not recall any of the movements. But lucy did.

Lucy drops the conversation and benjmain gets its jst without having to explore to her for so0kem actions only because he did not know himself.

The very next morning Benjamin wakes once again he is up on the apartments roof practicing the spiritual ways of the dark horse lucy was soon to arrive with the raven on her shoulder as she had won him too. In stead of the thought of him.

ready to answer Benjamin he continued that benjmain had brought him nothing but trouble. Benjamin answers here.
The raven continued that he was there to protect him and that was all. With those words ending the raven blasts Benjamin with a fierce circle of fire.
New powers Benjamin asks.

Lucy shouts to him that she had found them in her sleep, she had confused the both of them as she continued to stand another blast from the ravens mouth and beak. The power is towards benjmain as she answers again missing the conversation completely she continued as Benjamin tells her the answers his first question was that was the circle of fire for its spell of protections for a prayer before battle I will weave it every time faster than they ever can.

Chapter 13

Benjamin calls on the dark horse where was his special protector, his protection his special protection the dark horses explains that Lucy was still on their side Benjamin totally forgetting gets to understand they meet again side by side then begin the dark horse says you will fully understand.

The end

A CIP catalogue record for this title is available from the British Library.

Chapter One